Sly as a Foxe,

with Justice for Luke

By

Kim Beltz

Dedication

This book is dedicated to two handsome men. Luke Dutton, I will see that smile one day, but not today. Jason Beghe, maybe one day a meet and greet will be obtained, but not today.

Jen is my beautiful niece that was my crutch. Kevin for helping me with the detective work. Karina for telling me she wants to be there to sign my first copy. Mike for being my support even when I messed up, you were there.

To believe in myself and loving myself and putting on my big girl pants on and moving forward in this cruel world.

Kim Beltz

Table of Contents

Chapter One

We buried mom and dad today along with King their dog. Dad passed away 11 years prior, and we kept his ashes as per their wish, when the other one passed, we would bury them together, but they also wanted me to bury their dog King with them as well. It was a sad day, but it was a day of rejoicing because Mom would no longer be in pain. Going through her stuff for the next couple of months, I sat and got more depressed. Dad told me on his death bed, "Kid you will have your hands full when I am gone," and yes, he was right. However, Dad didn't realize how much it affected me as a child. Looking over an 8 ½ x 17 piece of paper that was filled out on 1 ½ pages of mom's medical history starting in 1957 to 2021. This poor woman suffered 4 miscarriages, a hysterectomy at the age of 32, 4 nervous breakdowns, 17 electro-shock treatments, in a coma from taking the wrong medication which resulted in having vocal cord damage that was done from the intern taking out the tube to fast and collapsing her windpipe, that resulted in a reconstruction of her vocal cords. We doctored that problem until 5 months before she passed, and 34 surgeries.

My childhood was so topsy turvey, I felt like a ping pong ball being bounced back and forth from grandparent to grandparents and then back to mom and dad. So as a child, I had to grow up fast and be an adult before I could be a child.

My childhood had its problems as well, but I look back and think how lucky I was, maybe I had a guardian angel. I rolled out of a moving car and rolled down and embankment in those days seat belts weren't mandatory, no damage except scrapped knees. At the age of 11 I went to a girlfriend's birthday party which included the adults supervising and it was a hot summer day, so we went swimming, a storm was rolling in, so we were all told to get out of the pool. The parents were in a travel trailer playing cards and they yelled for someone to bring them sodas, so I did. With a wet bathing suit, barefoot, and sodas in hand I stepped in a puddle of water where the electric cord was hooked up to the trailer from the house and lightning hit me. Flying toward the trailer it was like I was a magnet, and the cans were blown out of my arms and found the next day a block away. I was clinically dead but not mentally my father unplugged the trailer and jumped in the back seat of a car, giving me CPR, a block away from the hospital which was about 5 minutes away, he couldn't get me going, so he held me up by the scruff of my neck and cold-cocked me with his fist into my chest, and that is when he jumped started my heart. The doctor told them that one more minute and I would have been dead. I had to go to a psychiatrist because I was withdrawn socially, and anytime it thundered I trembled and cried. I was an A student prior but I declined to a C and D and sometimes even failed tests. It was like I couldn't comprehend what I would read but show me and I picked up so fast. Oh, and you think it couldn't get worse, well at the age of 12 I got raped by a cousin. I never told anyone because I felt no one would believe me. Is this why I didn't have a boyfriend in High School? So, when someone took an interest in me, I grabbed the first thing, oh yeah, I was a virgin still at the age of 21. Yeah, you never hear of that in this day and age. I dated this man for 4 years and I got married at the age of 24. I should have divorced him a year into the marriage because he physically abused me by throwing a can of vegetables at my head and to this day I have a nice scar above the right eye, just because I tickled him. He made me lie to my mother and father when I showed up to the house with a black and blue eye, by saying I ran into the cranked window of the trailer. The abuse went from physical to verbal and I last 32 years and I just couldn't take it anymore. WHAT AN IDIOT I WAS!

During this wonderful marriage, I worked two jobs to help support us, maybe I did this to stay away from the abuse. The second job was one of the best jobs I ever had. It was a party plan where I would demonstrate Christmas items. But I had to hear about that job, and he downgraded me for having that job, because I would never amount to anything. Well, I proved him wrong, one of the incentives was to not only earn money but trips as well. These trips weren't in the United States but the world. I travelled and took him too. Caribbean Cruises, Alaskan Cruise, Mexican Cruise, Hawaii, Egypt, Africa, Bali, Singapore, Italy, Greece, Spain Australia, New Zealand, Germany Switzerland and more.

I was very successful at this job, and I loved it. These are places that you can only dream about it, but I had an adventure on everyone. Yes, I took him with me even though he degraded me. I couldn't handle it anymore, so I sat Mom down and said Mom I have something to tell you, it was like I was going to the principal's office to tell her I was getting a divorce. "Mom, I wanted to tell you I am getting a divorce," and out of her mouth, came, what the hell took you so long. I guess you are never too old enough to learn new tricks! While still going through mom's belongings the days got darker and more depressing, and everything seemed jumbled in my brain. Flip-flopping back from good days as a child to the bad. Marriage not successful and did I waste 32 years? Getting deeper and deeper into depression. When married I decided to look for someone who might treat me better, I found this man and I left and moved in right away with him, the same way pattern I did when I moved out with my parents. I moved out at the age of 21, slept on my boyfriend's parents couch for 3 months till I found my own place. Then moved into an apartment with my boyfriend immediately, and he became my ex, then left my ex and moved in with my niece for 3 months but had my boyfriend live with me right away, moved mom out of her house that she insisted that I move in, and she moves into an assistant living, which she moved into 3 different facilities later. I moved mom out I moved in than moved my boyfriend in right away with him all within 3 months. So, 4 moves in less than 3 months, all while working, no I didn't lose my shit. I was never alone for any time; I don't know if I could be by myself.

Jobs, well that is a story in itself. My father chose my career when I was in High School.

Dad, I want to be a helicopter pilot - "NO"

Dad, I want to be a police officer - "NO"

Dad, I want to be a park ranger - "NO"

Well, dad what do you want me to do? "Go to school to be a dental assistant," so I did. Did I graduate NO, but I got a job in that field, 12 years in that profession. Then went to start a program for the billing department of IU students who had behavioral problems, then went to another company that started the same program. Then went to a radio station where I was a DJ for live remotes, and also sold advertising for the radio, then went to the local newspaper company and worked in the print department. Opened my own restaurant with a partner and the partnership didn't work, I worked 16-hour days and 7 days a week, whereas the partner worked 7-hour weeks. That dissolved fast because the ex said he would help, and he lasted 2 weeks and then quit on me but I lasted 7 months. Went back to the newspaper and worked as a newspaper ad agent. Then went to work for Minuteman Press selling print again, then Lowe's for 12 years and then bullied by the manager and fired, then now I am working at Mack Trucks. So yeah, I had a bunch of jobs, but I was proud of myself because every job was better than the one before and I had an interest in all. The last job my guardian angel my dad got me that job, he worked there, so he was looking out for me. Now I am being laid up for a bus accident which I will tell that story later.

Days still weren't getting better the nights raced in my head. The mental health issues of my family always were etched in my brain. Suicide and strange deaths were in our family. My great-grandmother shot herself, was it because of depression, I think so. That is because she buried two sons in one month. My grandfather's brother shot my grandfather in a hunting accident by mistake, his brother was so distraught that he fell into a hot furnace of zinc at the local Palmerton Zinc Company, all within one month. A cousin came home from Vietnam and didn't want to return to duty, so he ran a garden hose from the exhaust into the window of his car, lit a cigarette and the car exploded. My mom and Aunt had a lot of medical issues. Another cousin hung himself. Then another cousin was under a car and the jack slipped and crushed him, did it slip, or did he kick it out? I could never do anything to myself no matter how bad it would get because the living are the ones that suffer the most.

Children, well that was out of the question, my ex was selfish he didn't want any, so we never brought it up, and I followed mom in the hysterectomy at the age of 35. So, there was so much that I missed out on, no children, no grandchildren and the list goes on and on. My health was like my mother I just was so happy that I didn't follow in the footsteps of suicide like so many of the other family members. I was strong, but then COVID hit after mom and I never felt so confused and didn't care about anything in my life it was like I was another person. I can't explain, I just didn't care.

My boyfriend and I were sleeping in different rooms, not having sex all the time and it was the same thing day after day. We went hunting together, but no big trips, I was falling into a rut. I wasn't myself; my mind wasn't comprehending the good things in life that I had, it felt like I was in a spiral downhill motion, yes, I was getting depressed, wake up, don't do this. But I did, I just didn't care who I hurt, but I needed to feel alive and loved.

Chapter Two

WE PLAN AND GOD LAUGHS

WHITE OUT – NEED A CASE

NEVER DID I EXPECT TO PLAN MY LIFE OUT LIKE THIS, OR TELL MY STORY

MEMORIES OF HOW THEY SAY THE GOOD THE BAD AND THE UGLY.

CLIFF NOTES***NOT THE STORY AS OF YET! ***

Today I went to Wally world aka Walmart with a purpose to buy a journal that I could write my story and I found this journal that said on the outside. "Be kind to yourself". How appropriate! The first person that must feel better is myself. I made a huge mistake and hurt a lot of people. But the first person that I must heal is myself and fall in love with is myself, apologize to the people that I hurt, and if they can except me that I made a mistake and love me for me, because I am human, then I can't dwell but move on. For my mistake, I am owning up to it and making it right. One day at a time. I will have to live with this mistake till the day I die, but I must live life to the fullest. For tomorrow is never promised.

Definition for Addiction: the fact or condition of being addicted to a particular substance, thing or activity:

*Alcohol

*Sex

*Gambling

*Mine was falling for a scammer not once but twice. GOD, I WAS AN IDIOT!

Low self-esteem refers to a person having an overall poor sense of self-value and opinion of yourself.

So, when someone gives a person attention with low self-esteem that person gravitates to another. Saying things like your beautiful, you kind-hearted, I would love to spend the rest of my life with you, you make my heart skip a beat, I want to make love to you, we will travel, dance when there is no music, take showers together, hold hands, go for walks, go for rides, and the list goes on to make you feel like a queen. THAT IS THE FIRST SIGN OF A SCAMMER WHEN HE CALLS YOU HIS QUEEN, THEY SAY THAT BECAUSE THEY HAVE SO MANY OTHER CONVERSATIONS THAT THEY FORGET YOUR NAME AND CALL YOU QUEEN.

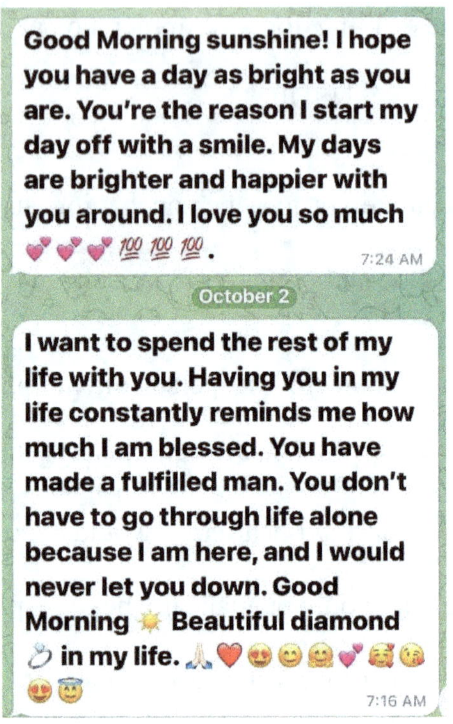

However, the first mistake I made was I never confronted my boyfriend and told him how I felt, that was a huge mistake. This person never deserved what I did, but like I said I was in a dark place, and I didn't care who I hurt. But it wasn't fair to him.

Chapter Three

So, jumping to a year and a half ago. I wasn't looking for anything, but I got a friend request from this gentleman named "George Foxe." Looking at his pictures online before I accepted, I thought who the hell is this handsome man with the smile that would melt any woman's heart? His body was that of a bodybuilder and his eyes could reach into your soul.

Ok, Kim stop drooling.

His profile said he was from Germany, and he was divorced and now single. Hmmm! So, I accepted, the 1st mistake, if they were that good what the hell did, he want with me as a friend? Ok, so I accepted.

What the hell, conversations don't hurt, 2nd mistake. Go on messenger and we can talk, 3rd mistake. Oh, but the cuteness was there. Hi how are you doing, my name is George.

It was like the Jerry Mcquire movie, "You Got Me from HELLO," boom I was a teenager with a crush. I even went to my niece's ex-husband and asked him to run the phone number. Aunt Kim don't do it is a scam. Did I freaking listen, NO this isn't true, he loves me, he said.

We talked about the day, the days turned into weeks, with everything that he said swept me off my feet. It was how he was saying it. Everything that a smooth talker could say to hook your line and sinker, the romance through texts. I love you; I can't imagine my life without you, I want to dance with you, hold hands, stand behind you and kiss your neck, turn you around and kiss your sweet lips. Oh god what have I done, I fell hard, the text message continued of the lovemaking and the feeling of satisfaction of being a woman again.

We got closer, he showed me his divorce papers and he showed me pictures of his son and him. His son was a law student going to a college in Austin Texas, not far from his home in Texas. His job was a mechanical engineer and he worked for companies like Exxon on oil rigs. He showed me his driver's license and I just looked at the handsome man on it and never looked at it closely.

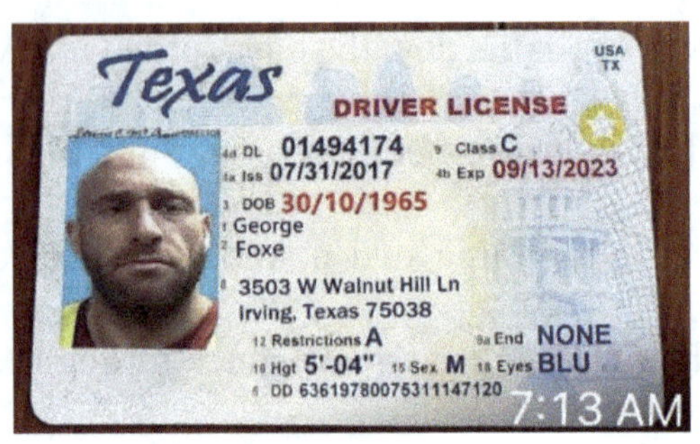

Kim, I got a job, and I am leaving at the end of the week, I got a job with Exxon in Canada, and I need help, this will be our future, help me we will be partners, and this will benefit us, so our life cannot be a dream but a reality. So, I gave in, I helped with the plane ticket.

For the documents that I need to do the job, I need to have a lawyer go over them and present them and the insurance company to cover them, please help me. I promise this will be the last, oh can you please send me money for data and food?

I need money for the helicopter to get from land to the rig.

I need money for the equipment, the bill is going to be in the

thousands of dollars, but I promise this will be the last. Oh, by the way I love you. Life is going to be so wonderful when we are together, how did God give me such a caring and loving woman that works together and loves her man.

Oh my God, the red flags should have gone up, they were there, and the money was sent with gift cards, wire transfers, bitcoin, and Cash App, what the hell was I doing? I didn't care.

Hun, oh my God, I am hurt. Hun, you need to help me the police that are on the rig have me I am in the hospital on the rig. I am hurt. How George what happened. I got in a fight because I didn't have the money to pay one of the men who worked for me, I needed to pay him so they would look at my injuries. George sent me pictures, his face was marked up and his leg was badly bruised, they did an x-ray of his leg and he sent it to me. His leg was scattered. Oh my God, I needed to make this right, I need to help him. I paid the man what George owed him, I paid for the medical needs, I paid for him to be

transferred to a hospital on land to have his operation.

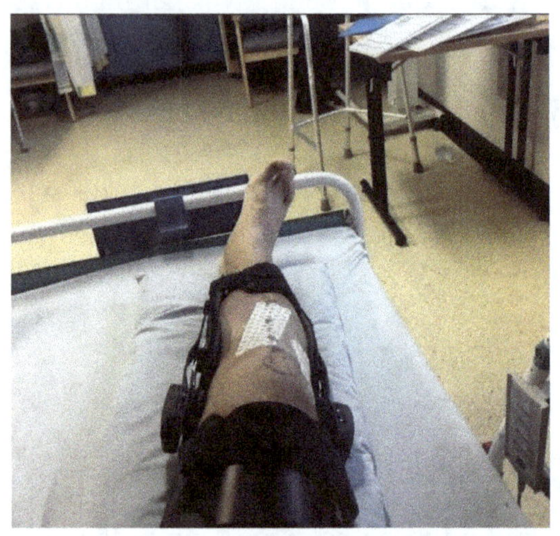

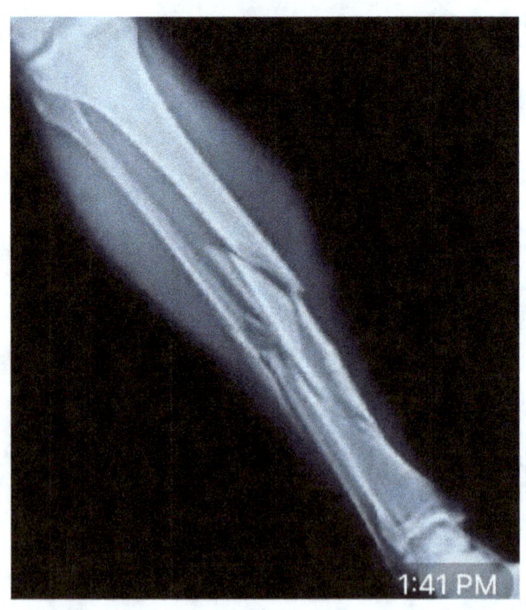

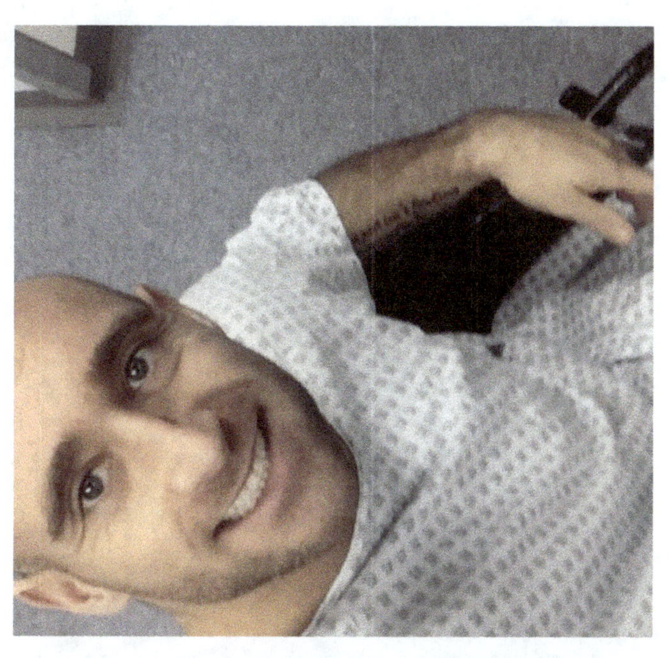

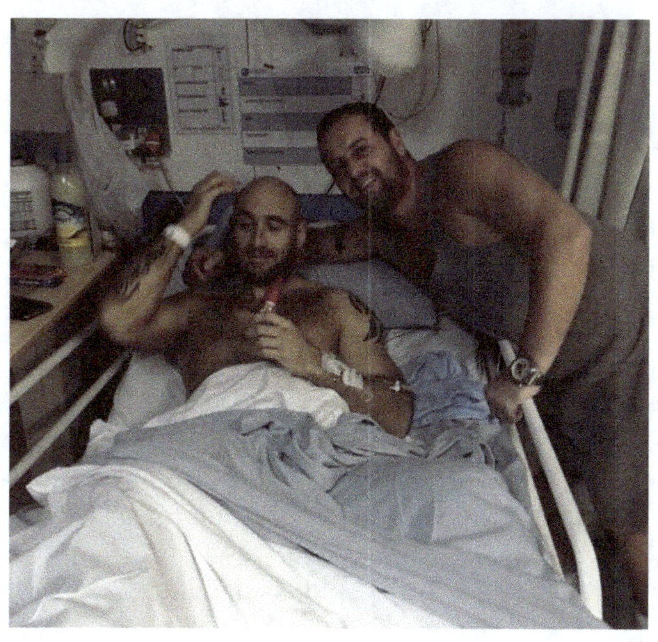

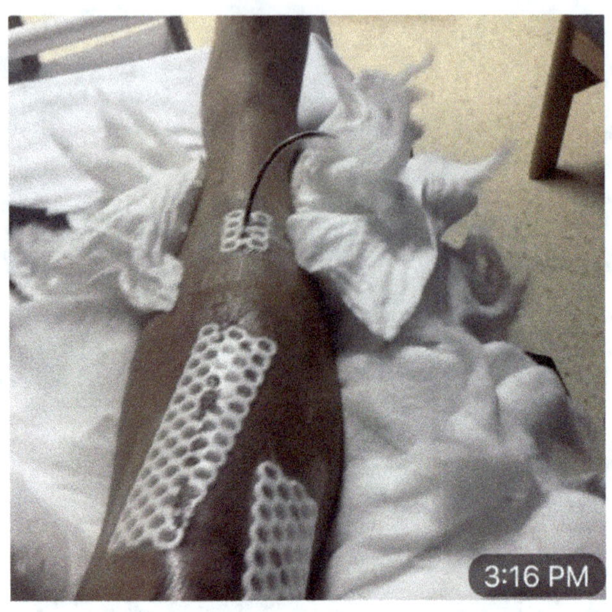

Oh my God, let me be with you please I will fly up and take care of you, no Hun please don't I love you and you need to be strong for both of us. How did this man break your leg? The man broke my leg using a crowbar, and I couldn't fight back. He was beating me, and he hurt me so badly.

George had the operation, with a tube coming out of his ankle to drain the blood so that he wouldn't get a blood clot. I saw pictures of him in the hospital bed, with a brace that went from his ankle to way over his knee almost to his groin. I felt so alone and so hurt that I couldn't help. I will be coming home soon, and we will be together. How about we live in Denver Colorado? Oh, George, that sounds nice. How about you look at houses and I will contact my realtor and we will decide what we want. Ok, that sounds lovely. I think we should get a ranch-style home because of your injury George, what do you think? Sounds like a plan, why don't you look and show me what you would like because I want my future wife to be happy.

How does this one look hun, or this one, this one is a development, and these are the parks for the dogs, and it has 3 bedrooms so when your son comes to visit, we can make the one room into an office for you. Oh, Kim, it is perfect. I will make arrangements and we will put a bid on it with the realtor, please make sure you talk to your financial advisor so we can do a wire transfer, so we don't lose it, till we get paid from Exxon. Ok, George, I will make arrangements, I can't wait to see you. The relator called and the amount for the bid is $30k

please do a wire transfer. Alright, George.

RECENTLY VIEWED PLANS

3 BEDS | **3** BATHS | **1698** SQ FT # 041-00295

Chapter Four

Hun, I can't wait any longer when I get home, I want to get married immediately and make mad passionate love to you. Please send me money, so that we can get the 4 million released that I am owed and a flight ticket to the closest airport. George, I don't have that kind of money anymore, you drained everything, my inheritance, both my 401 K and I racked up my credit cards to the max. I will take care of it honey when I get home. How much do you have? I only have enough money for the hotel and the flight home. Ok send me the money and when we get married, we will go for a loan and get that money that is owed from us from EXXON.

George, can you please send me the flight schedule, I will do better than that I will send you a copy of the airline ticket. How are you making out with the wedding arrangements? I will pick you up at the airport, the hotel room is paid for a week, I called the courthouse, and we can file for the marriage license on Tuesday, pick it up on Friday and the minister is booked. Not telling George that I had a horse-drawn carriage booked in the town of Bethlehem, with the minister marrying us on this beautiful ride as we drove around Bethlehem, PA. It was going to be magical only a couple of weeks before Christmas and the whole town was decorated; to top it off it was to have snow falling. What a fairy princess tale.

I was excited, I packed the whole car without the boyfriend knowing and I left to go to the hotel, I had just enough of the car packed that I could get George's items in for his trip home to our new house in Colorado. I called the boyfriend and left him know that I was leaving and not coming home, not telling him the whole story just that I needed to be alone. I blocked all calls from everyone I loved including my niece.

Oh my God the day arrived, and I was sitting in the airport patiently waiting for the man of my dreams to walk down the airport hallway. Minutes turned into an hour, the last flight into ABE landed and no George. Crying on the way back to the hotel, which was decorated for Christmas, with wine in the fridge, and two wine goblets on the coffee table with candles and rose petals all over the bed. I busted into tears. Threw myself on the bed still dressed and cried myself to sleep. What the hell did I do? Where was George? I left voice messages and no answer from George. I was a mess I need to go home.

I went home and sucked it up. The boyfriend helped me unpack and still not telling him what went on, I kept the secret. I secretly went into a room and cancelled the minister and the wedding.

Twenty – four hours turned into Forty – eight and then I heard from George. I was held up in the airport and they found cocaine in my backpack, with my injury you know I couldn't put the bags in the cab, the cab driver planted. I was then taken away and they put a blindfold on me and now I am somewhere overseas in an ARAB, speaking country. DING, DING, DING, light bulb finally went off. What the hell George then why do you have your phone, if you were a goddamn hostage you wouldn't be texting me. I am sorry but I don't believe you. Here is proof, they took a picture of me with some others and here is the picture they made me send to you.

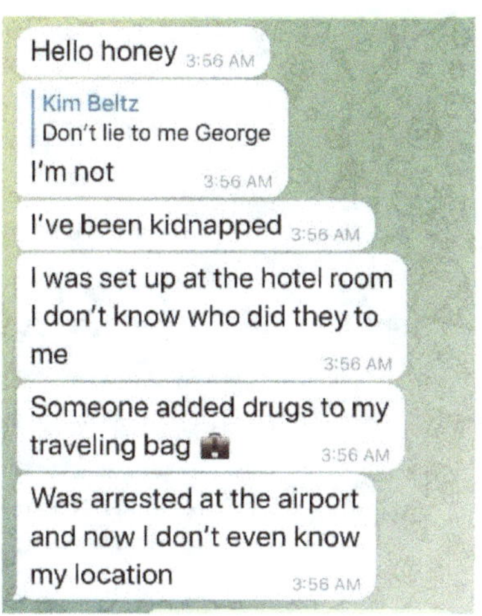

George, are you fucking crazy, this picture is photo shopped and with your leg, there is no freaking way that you would be kneeling. So lay off the crap, the lies need to stop. I am done. This went on for weeks, but I didn't send any money. Remarkable he got back in Canada.

35

Honey, please pay for me to get home it is only 300. I lost my VISA, and I must get home to make this right to you. I am ready to go, omg it was only 300 not thousands of dollars, ok I will give in. So, I sent the 300. What about cab money, data, and meds I need another 200. Oh that 300 is not the equivalent I need 175 more. OMG, the 300 turned into 600 plus. LIES!

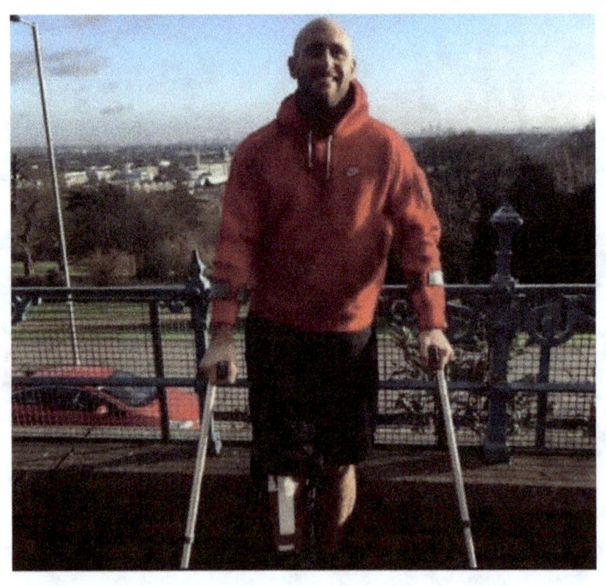

I had enough! I was done with the lies. So, I stopped but the texts still came in. I need money for VISA, I need money for data, I need money for food, I am starving to death. How can you treat your husband this way, I need money for meds. It is only 60 dollars. Yeah bullshit, you stripped me out of my inheritance George. Honey, I have a friend that is sending you money. Please accept it. Wow, I got two checks, maybe this was true, close to 70k.

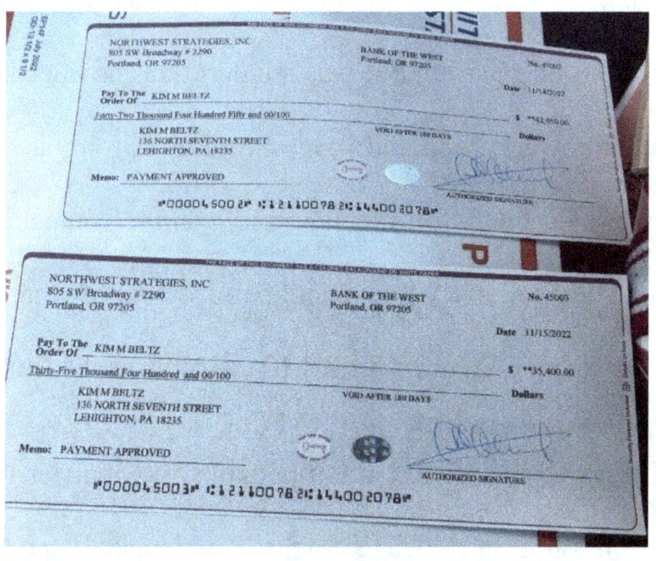

I went to the bank and cashed them, and the bank gave me 4K in advance. Send me that and I will be able to come home, and we can get married. So, I did, went down to the airport waited again, but this time I didn't make any arrangements until I saw him get off the plane. Guess what no show. George, you son of a bitch, I texted him you God damn stood me up again. Where the hell are you. I am still in Canada, and they wouldn't let me go through customs without my ID. I have someone that can get me through, but it will be so much. God damn it, George. I went home and I got a notification on my phone it was an alert that the checks that he gave me were fraud and I was overdrawn in my account. You son of a bitch you did it to me again. I contacted my financial advisor, and I took enough money out of what I had left to cover the overdraft fee. OMG, which was the last.

I dropped his ass like a hot potato. I was madder than a hornet on a hot tin roof. His texting was blocked, and I was still angry, brokenhearted and financially in ruin. What the fuck was I going to do, the credit card companies were being hard ass with me they wanted their payment. Ok so I called a hardship company, and they took over the payments, with the Prudential check that I got monthly I only had to come up with

60 a month for the next 5 years. I could handle that, I than got my act together and refinanced out a loan and paid off a loan and other stuff that was outstanding and putting the house up for collateral. I made a mistake; I am stepping up and pulling my big girl pants on and handling this on my own. With what I made at Mack Trucks I could do this no sweat. I could work another 10 years, take retirement, sell the house pay off the loan and still had money to live in a tiny house in Florida and live my life in peace, I thought.

Chapter Five

Well, George wasn't contacting me, and I was facing up to my horrible life choices. I was finally on the right path. Then flipping through social media again on Facebook I saw an actor that I thought would be neat to do a meet and greet. What an idiot again. This actor is a well-known celebrity and is on a weekly TV show on Wednesday nights and is very handsome and two years older than I am. How cool so I made a friend request from him, and he accepted without hesitation.

Talking back and forth the meet and greet was thousands of dollars and he wanted them on gift cards again. Ding, Ding, Ding another scammer, what the hell was I a fly that was drawn into the sugar bowl? Two third in the morning I received three FaceTime phone calls from the scammer, a Nigerian man, no famous actor. I had enough of this shit. How do I catch these scammers. Well, I looked up this actor managers and yes, he did meet and greets and the money for them go to charities. Ok so I contacted his manager, and I figured I would contact a female. Her name is Lisa, female to female, I explained to her what happened with Jason, and I thought he should be aware of what was transpiring and ruining his name.

Lisa marber Rich private page
Business chat
↩ Lisa marber Rich private page replied to you

Have you heard
from Jason

She said she was going to reach out to him and explain what was going on. Lisa and I talked for days and then she told me that Jason wanted to talk to me and that I should download an app called Telegram. So, I did and she said that he would give me an IP address and to contact him on this app. So I did. Jason and I started talking and we hit it off. His birthday was coming up and he asked me if I was going to do something special for him. So I told him I didn't have much money and would surprise him, so I did a video count down 5 days before his birthday. Everyday new video and signing happy birthday with a different message every day. It was fun and he told me it was the nicest gift he ever got. But the day after his birthday I got the nicest video message from him, saying to me that he thought that I was so special and that he wanted to come and get me and he wanted to start dating. I told him how are we going to do this he told me to send him 600 and to pay for a plane ticket and the meet and greet would be worked out.

He would take care of the hotel and we would be together. We were connecting he told me about his entire life, from his divorce from his wife, because she filed asking why, he said he had dinner with a costar and his wife took it out of context. She wouldn't go to therapy to save their marriage, and not to make it hard for the boys he didn't fight.

He told me about how he got of Scientology, and he was outcast from the group because he talked about the situation. He explained the pyramid structure and he gave me more details and the biggest reason he got out was because the organization didn't want him to have a family life, and he loved his boys too much. He would send me voice messages telling me how he was excited in getting together and how much he cared for me.

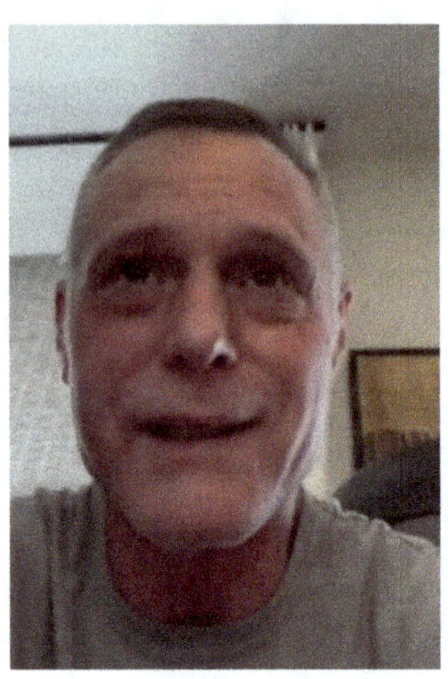

He was single for so long and he was finally trusting again

and he trusted me to the moon and back.

We talked about his dogs, his pug, Jack and his other dog

Nitro. The next-door neighbours would walk them for him and

when he went away, they would keep them until he got back.

He had a personal cook for 10 years who became a friend, and

her name was Emily. She made BBQ salmon for him, lasagna,

and other meals. Breakfast would be coffee and Cheerios or

eggs and bacon and he loved pancakes. He would leave for

work at 9 and arrive at 10, he would text me when he left and would text me when he arrived. Telling me about his daily activities, from voiceovers to reviewing contracts for the upcoming season to doing interviews for new hires for the show. He would text me when he left work and get home.

Working until 3 or 4, coming home, taking a nap, and getting up to eat what Ms. Emily made for him. We would text and have voice messages, and conversations. Easter was around the corner, and he was going out to the boys. He told me that the house in California had a tennis court and he and the boys were going to play chess and they had a concert picked out for them to go to, but he backed out because he was tired, and wanted to talk to me instead of the loud music. He informed me that the boys weren't told about me that he wanted to make it a surprise and he informed me that I didn't have to worry, they would love me as much as he loved me. I told him that I would never replace their mother but that I wanted to be a part of their life as well and that I hoped they would accept me. Easter arrived and I asked where he was going to eat, and he had made reservations at an Italian

Restaurant. Two days later he flew back from LA to Chicago.

Chapter Six

Jason got back to Chicago and then it started getting weird again, he was showing his temper, getting angry at the producers and told me that they froze his assets and to open his accounts, and to get them to unfroze he needed 70K, I told him I would bring out the check to him and then we would go to the bank together and make this right. No, was the answer I got, and I started arguing with him more and more, Lisa jumped in and told me that I should support my husband in his time of need.

All of a sudden I didn't hear from him in Chicago, for two days, getting in contact with Lisa and saying I was scared that I didn't hear from him I got a message from her at 1 in the morning. Don't get alarmed but Jason is fine, he was in the hospital the whole weekend being observed because he fell and hit his head getting out of the shower. Lisa I am coming out. No Kim, he told me to tell you to hang in there and he will call you. The next night I heard from Jason, and we texted into the wee hours of the morning. I told him I was coming out to take care of him, and he refused and told me he would be ok. Then a week later Monday I received a message from him stating that he was getting on a private plane to Dubai, regarding a business arrangement that he had, and he wanted me to review the paperwork and let me know what I found out.

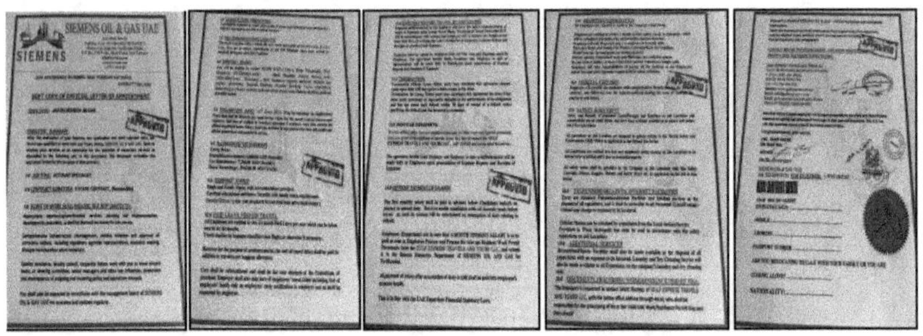

Well, here we go again, an oil company. The address was wrong, the CEO already retired two years prior, and the web address was made up. OMG, another scam. Jason get home now; this is a scam, and they are going to take you over. Kim,

I can't I took the money and deposited it already and now with my account froze I can't get it out. Jason what are you going to do. Kim I am going to be home this weekend come out to see me, and we will make this right, bring your check book. I will pick you up at the airport in the meantime mail the 70K to this address Scott Rose in Huntington NY. Well, I called my bank, this was sounding to much like a repeat scam to me.

Good afternoon Truist Bank, hi this is Kim, is Karina there? No, she isn't. If I wrote a check can I cancel it before it is cashed? Yes, you can, and the fee would be $35.00. Well, I cancelled a check before I wrote it out, this was the best $35.00 I spent. Well, the 70K was written out and sent out the package overnight and with a signature required. Well, the next day I boarded the plane but while I was taxiing on the tarmac, Jason sent me a text that he wouldn't be home and I should get off the plane. It was too late the plane was in the air to Chicago. Got off the plane and texted back and forth and I rearranged my flight and flew back to Philadelphia the same day. While on the bus from the airport to the parking lot shuttle the bus driver rounded a corner to fast and it threw me out of the seat hitting my head on the back of the seat and slammed my back and right hip. The bus driver didn't even stop but the passengers picked me up, my Edralin was pumped, and I didn't feel it till the next day, I was tired, and couldn't keep my eyes open and I hurt in my head and my whole body was aching. OMG, please take me to the ER. 14 hours later I was told that I had whiplash and that I could go back to work on lite duty.

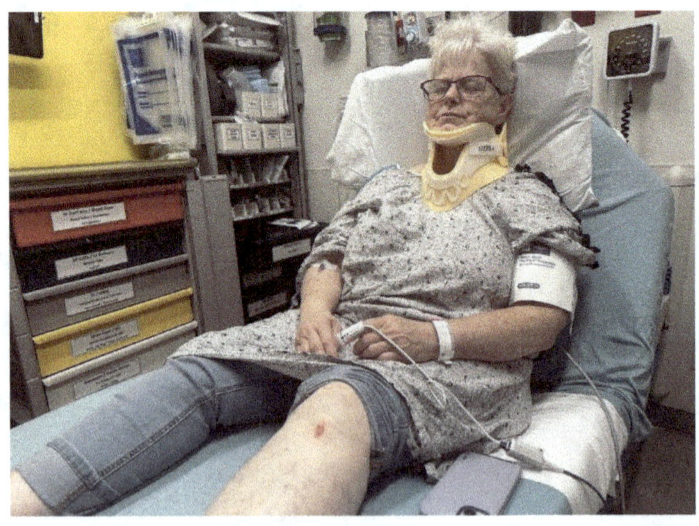

Went back to work and they told me to go to the doctor I am still off work, and I started doing my notes and research. What I found out is what is now the unveiling of how this world is so screwed up. You will be shocked as to what I am about to tell you, it will blow you away. So, hold onto your seat, and let me tell you what I am finding out.

Chapter Seven

The Lies and hurt, have me so pissed off I hate George Foxe and now I hated this Jason scumbag. If I had both in front of me, the rage would be ready to explode. I never slapped anyone, but I would slap both in the face. No, I would punch them in the nose and hope I did damage. The financial ruin they put me through. The lies on top of lies. Now I was so mad I was madder than that hornet on a hot tin roof again. Let me at them.

Ok, so I started out on a Saturday morning at the crack of dawn and then the face came on the app, I read about this George, OMG, no way. The tears started to pour.

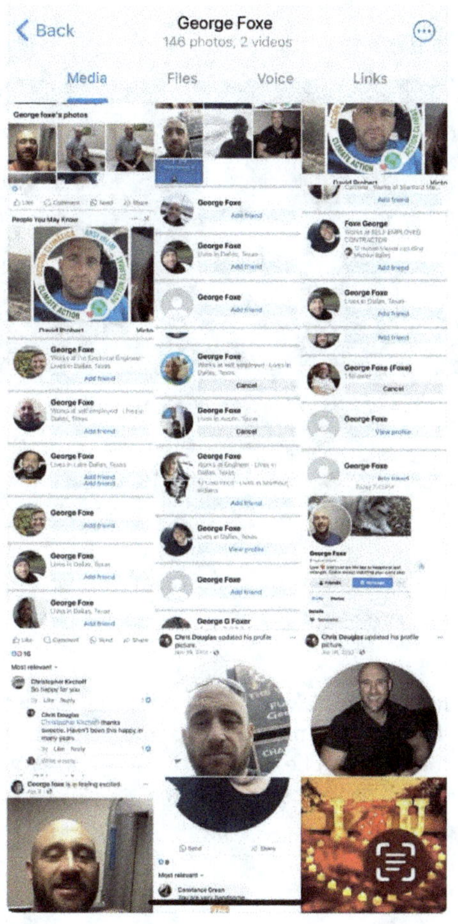

27 Facebook accounts with George Foxe and 15 other names with his photo, than a dozen or more under Luke Dutton, then an alert came on the app.

You Are Being Scammed
Oct 14, 2021 ·
Mobile uploads

Luke Dutton passed away in 2021 after a failed attempt at suicide. His stolen photos are used with his stolen name. You will never be talking to the real man. You will be talking to a heartless evil scammer.

Gail Colley and 5 others

I sat in aww, crying and crying, Luke Dutton died, and the scum bags stole his id and now they are destroying his name and memories but also his family and maybe he had a girlfriend. But this isn't fair. God, how can people get so cruel? Mom died on 10-25-21, and Luke committed suicide on 6-30-21 which was almost 4 months before her passing.

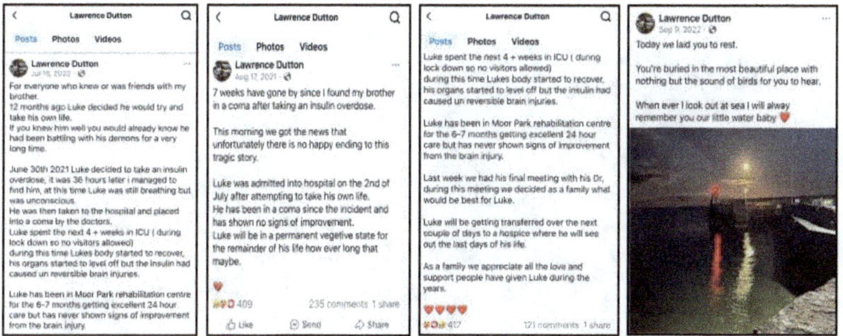

Luke Dutton was an engineer for oil rigs in the past, and a former bodybuilder who got into substance abuse and alcohol and was trying to get sober, but he also suffered mental health issues. I read his blogs on Facebook, Instagram, and TikTok. This beautiful man that I fell in love with, now I was understanding his life. This was not Luke's fault.

Luke tried to commit suicide and it failed, this is where the broken leg came into play, he tried to jump off a building, but it failed. The pictures were real. He then went into body building again and got tattoos for his journey. "Even the best fall sometimes", tattooed across his fine chiseled chest and on his left forearm. "The hardest part isn't finding what we need to be, it's being content with who we are."

From there he got help and accepted that he had a problem, was sober and was also being a mentor. "Who loved ice cream at 7 am on the porch outside his house on a sunny morning?"

He was getting his life in order when he had a snap and tried to commit suicide again, but this time he took an overdose of insulin and laid in his apartment for a couple of days without any brain activity and was in a vegetable state, this lasted over a year, then the family decided to let Luke rest in Peace. This smile was no longer going to grace his mother or brother or the family that he left behind. So now I am on a quest to have justice not only for myself but for Luke. This process is not going to be done overnight however it will be a project that I am going to try to hand over to Kevin, my niece's ex-husband that is a detective and hopefully the FBI.

I have email addresses that were used under all names, I have the ID # of Facebook accounts, and I have messenger address.

I have fraud check routing numbers and account numbers, I have wire transfer numbers as well. Telephone numbers, email addresses from couriers, Badge # Driver's licenses, Bitcoin addresses.

Airline Ticket numbers and receiver of checks that I was the middleman to mail. My account amounts that were spent.

Jason's emails, phone #, the receiver of the 70K check and so much more. Jason's reputation was shattered as well, from his manager's reputation to the list goes on and on.

I watched a movie last night by myself, and it hit home so hard, The Beekeeper, watch it, not only does it deal with the scum bags, but it also shows how these people make this their job that works for companies that do this to innocent people. It also showed what can happen when this happens to the innocent, suicide, depression and also how people are now trying to stop this from happening.

My advice is to enjoy what you have, you worked too hard to give it to someone else, and if it sounds too good to be true, it probably is. I made an appointment today to get two tattoos I wanted to copy Luke's but the pain would be with me forever, so I decided to get one that reads, "Just breathe" with a picture of a dandelion and the seedlings blowing in the wind, and the other a lavender sprig with the words, "let it go", placed on either side of my arms that when I look at them, I realize that I must go on.

Be happy with yourself and who you are, you are beautiful, and remember, God Loves you and so do I. I look forward to the day when I can meet Luke and Jason to tell them their story and to tell them I worked hard for justice for us all. But my day is not today to meet Luke, I must live and laugh and smile again, my journey will be hard, but I will survive. What is the saying "I am woman hear me roar", well look out world ROAR!

Conclusion and Findings

When I got angry at myself and thought how stupid I was, I starteddoing research and this is what I found on an app that allows you to scan anyone's face and it comes up with an ID.

I first went on Facebook and searched and typed in George Foxe -27 plus ID's came up with his face. ID ME app came up with the real name of Luke Dutton and I did Facebook search and there were 15 plus of that name. There were other names with the photo as well.

Checking every post and picture, I finally found the right Luke Dutton who passed away 4 months prior to me talking to George Foxe that thescammers stole his id.

My Facebook account got hacked, but it was George Foxe's nameit was under, and I pinned pointed the account and the following pictures of the people that were on that account. There were two gentlemen that attended a Trading seminar and guess what??? The money was always done to the Canadian currency, and this is what I found on this account, and the saying "When you no longer care what happens", wow that is exactly what scammers believe, we don't care who we hurt, but we need to get more.

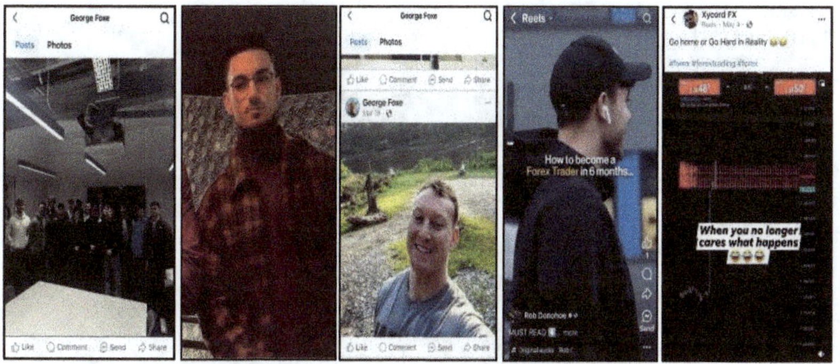

Similarities with George and Jason:

Broken leg – George was through fighting, Jason was a car accident in Dubai, that they both wanted me to pay the hospital bills. Here are Jason's fake photos:

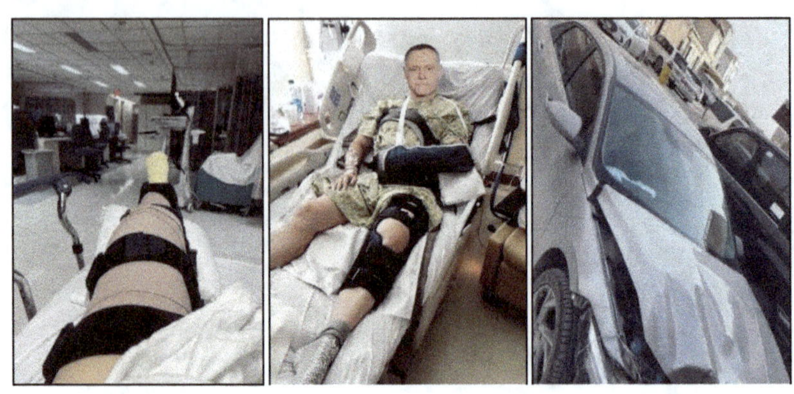

Blood oaths for marriage

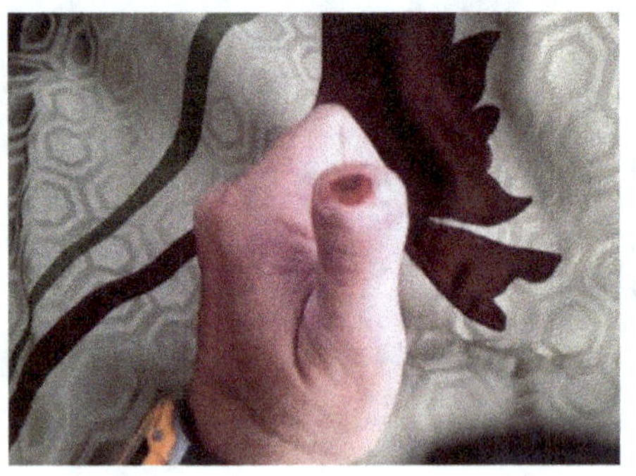

George's driver's license, DOB was formatted incorrectly. Addresswas for a female driver. George told me he was close to 6', driver's license was 5'4".

Oil rig picture was a taken from an oil rig that was taken out of commission.

Airport picture of George was photoshopped.

Jason's, Dubai contract was so fake that if the paper could catch on fire it would have from all the lies on it. Person signed it retired twoyears prior, address was fake, telephone numbers were fake, web address fake, and the list goes on and on.

These are just a few items I found as I dug into finding out the truth. I know that this will be a long road ahead of me to find these scammers but writing this book is just a step in the right direction to self-healing for myself and for Justice for Luke. If I can help one person feel that they are not alone with scammers and that they can get anything out of this for themselves than I feel blessed that I can share my story.

Kim